THIS BOOK BELONGS TO

....

....

....

....

....

THANK YOU FOR CHOOSING OUR ALEBRIJE
COLORING BOOK!

YOUR CHOICE MEANS THE WORLD TO US, AND
WE'RE TRULY THANKFUL FOR YOUR SUPPORT.

WE'RE THRILLED TO JOIN YOU ON THIS
CREATIVE JOURNEY, AIMING TO BRING JOY,
FUN, AND COUNTLESS PRECIOUS MOMENTS TO
YOUR COLORING ADVENTURES.

IF YOU HAVE A MOMENT, WE WOULD BE
INCREDIBLY GRATEFUL FOR YOUR FEEDBACK.
PLEASE CONSIDER LEAVING A REVIEW TO
SHARE YOUR THOUGHTS.

HAPPY COLORING!

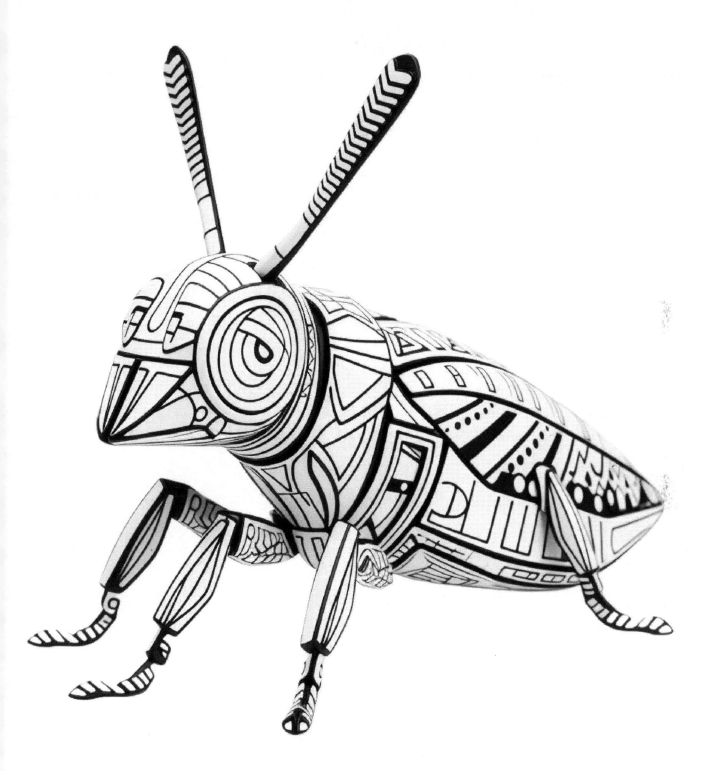

Made in the USA
Las Vegas, NV
01 February 2024